THE LIGHT OF THE MIND

THE LIGHT OF THE MIND

DEJAN STOJANOVIĆ

New Avenue Books

NOTE TO THIS EDITION

This collection of poems is the final book in the series titled *The Embrace of Light and Darkness* (a pentalogy) and represents their first publication in book form. The poems were originally written in English between 2005 and 2010, with some exceptions added or revised later.

D. S.

Contents

A STAR IN THE MIND
INNER SPACE

A STAR DEEP IN THE MIND

I see a new star on the horizon.

It's not a Morning Star;

It's a star without light.

The star without light is the brightest,

But its glow remains within.

The star without light is the largest,

But it doesn't occupy any space.

It exists within itself.

It nourishes all other stars

And the entire physical World.

Without space, there is no time.

Without time, there is no aging.

Without aging, there is no death.

The star without light never dies.

It cannot be seen in outer space,

But it can be sensed deep within the mind.

ISLAND

Dreams, flying out from the mind,
Become birds flying over the sea.

The Sun, sprouting from the sea,
Makes the sea blue.

The flying dream that hovers in space
Becomes an Island in the sea.

The Island—the dream from the mind,
The bird, the air, the sea, and the light.

INNER SPACE

To become a flying saucer,

Entering a cell and penetrating deep,

To find a new galaxy

Would be an honorable task

For a new scientist

More interested in the inner state

Of the soul than in outer space.

THE SOURCE

There exists a substance

Beyond mere materiality,

A mind that transcends physical matter.

It grows from within,

Follows its own path,

Nourished solely by the desire to live.

This is how matter is born,

How the first poet sings

The shamanic song,

How he romantically

Engages with nothingness

Using the flower of the mind,

Emerging from the Universal Source

Of Everything.

AFTERLIFE LIGHT

It is no longer present,
But we can still see it,
And you will see it
For millions of years to come.
Did the Star die? Did it live?
In life, we call this phenomenon
A ghost, a hallucination.
(Is life a ghost?)
What if the star never lived at all?
Or maybe death dies
While the star continues to live,
Cheating on death
With the afterlife light.

THE LIGHT FROM THE MIND

Morning fills the mind with light,

Inviting the world

On a journey through uncharted territory,

Where daisies awaken slowly and thrive longer

Thanks to spring's arrival in the desert.

In this garden stands a temple,

Bathed in the glow of light from within,

Opening a long path through the desert

For the world to discover its way

To land safely in your thoughts,

Glowing with a faithful light.

SEAGULL FROM FAR

Lie down on the ground and listen to the grass,

Soar high to catch the quiet signals

Of music from outer space,

Dream by creating and create by dreaming.

Become the thing you observe,

Feel what the trees, bathed in sunlight, experience.

Breathe in the world, not just the air.

Gaze far into the distance to see

The seagull emerging from the sea.

Imagine it as the birth of the world and greet it.

Welcome the old bird

That has flown from afar to meet you.

Fulfill your desire to fly, see, and be seen.

MEMORY AND OBLIVION

When everything is lost, there remains a memory
From which a new city will be built, a new world.
Those who have memory will be rich.

Oblivion heals old wounds; you must agree.
On the road, there is only the past and the future.
When everything is lost, there remains a memory.

Memory will save oblivion from bad dreams.
When the new city is built, it will become a temple bestowed
By those who have memory to make others wealthy.

In the center of the city, before the temple,
The keepers of the fire will all abide.
When everything is lost, there remains a memory.

From night, fire will be born
As new light when all knowledge is swallowed.
Those who have memory will be rich.

A new rose will bloom from the dark sea,
A city revived from memory and abode.
When all is but a memory, there remains a memory.
Those who have memory will be rich.

I REMEMBER THE SNOW IN THE SUMMER'S LIGHT

I remember the snow in the summer's light,
Thinking of summer in winter and of winter in summer.
When I see the blue, I know the white.

I see the haze over the rooftops bright
And feel the warm air caressed by the azure.
I remember the snow in the summer's light.

Summers were lazy in my inner sight;
Winters, lazy on the outside, were sure to secure
The blue when I felt the cold of the white.

Winter takes me on summer's flight
To visit the summer and to endure
The snows while remembering the light.

Maybe I like spring and fall the most,
But winter becomes spring in the summer to allure.
I feel the fall and see the blue in the white.

I keep remembering, seeing all bright—
Everything is just a thought you conjure.
I remember the snow hiding in the light;
When I see the blue, I know the white.

DON'T OBSTRUCT THE SUN

"Don't obstruct the Sun,"

Said Diogenes to the great man.

Even great men respect the wishes

Of those indifferent to power,

But close to the source,

Without whose help

Great men would blindly

Sit in darkness.

Even the great men bow before the Sun,

Which melts hubris into humility,

Making a human more human.

THE NEW SUN AND THE NEW MOON

EMBRACING A NEW DAY

Finding a way, when it seems there is none,

Feels impossible. Yet the world

Changes its appearance from time to time,

Following the trends of the moment.

It flirts with VIPs of all kinds:

Entrepreneurs, politicians,

Professors, scientists, and authors—

So-called famous people of every type.

While everything changes,

Some things remain constant,

The familiar world appears anew.

NEW HOME

She followed her thoughts,
Nourished by her dreams,
Unaware of her own self-realization,
Yet she understood the power of desire,
As it emerged from her dreams and transformed
Into clear thoughts and visions
Of what awaits her if she stays focused.
She knew that something was waiting,
Ready to embrace her dreams far ahead,
Once her thoughts demonstrated
Devotion and loyalty to those dreams.

It was the smiling dreams
That had been waiting for her all along.

A NEW FRIEND

Tell me something less significant—
Something about our biology, for example,
About unjustified failures,
Rather than fame and success.
Tell me what you hear while sitting under the tree,
Or share stories of lonely lions in the prairies.
Forget about decorated generals;
Tell me about Private Ryan instead.
Share something only you know,
And make a new friend.

THE NEW SUN AND THE NEW MOON

Too much has already been written

About the Sun and the Moon.

We have started to believe that both of them

Have somehow become new.

However, the Sun remains the same old Sun,

And the Moon is still the same old Moon.

While many things have changed

Among human beings and their affairs,

The Sun and the Moon have stayed the same.

THE SEA AND THE WORLD

The sea, the music, the morning.
While the world sleeps, the sea sings
Quietly about the path the world takes.
It sings from the depths, sending signals
For the world to find its way,
Spreading the scent of its mystery—
A song about its own enigma,
Reflecting on the meaning of shores,
Waiting for the world to arrive safely
In the harbor of silence.

THE WORLD IS NEITHER HAPPY NOR SAD

The world has suddenly become sad.

There is too much cheering,

Too much unsubstantiated hope.

Who would claim that

Everything could change overnight?

Hopes are merely dreams,

Evaporating much faster

Than they are built.

And we stand hypnotized,

Paralyzed by this sudden revelation,

Accusing the world and blaming our hopes,

Hoping to find another excuse

For yet another episode

Of postponed endings—

Of something that should have ceased long ago.

Even hopes have their limits.

In this new episode,

Actors must confront themselves

Instead of living in a dreamland.

The world remains neither sad nor happy.

INDIFFERENT WORLD

I struggle with words,
With visions, ideas, and imagination.
There is too much competition
Among them, and too little time
To experience them all, to see them all
Come to life in an indifferent world,
Equally indifferent to their existence.

LITTLE WORLD

Let's forget about important things today.

Let's focus on little things and use simple words.

For instance, let's sit in the garden.

Let's forget crowds and let go of our goals.

Let us become the goals we are trying to achieve.

Let us be small in a big world

And see if the world welcomes

Our desire to simply exist

Without too much pomp or pretension.

NEW WORLD

People talk about a New World Order,

But what if we could create a New World instead?

We need new horizons, not just cover-ups,

Not the same old system dressed up as new.

New horizons can inspire proper governance,

Fostering innovation and a just approach,

Creating fresh partnerships and opportunities.

This shift could mean fewer wars;

Even if it doesn't cultivate more love,

It could spark greater compassion,

Illuminating the path of awakened souls

To build a New Temple as a lighthouse,

Spreading light instead of darkness

Over the tiny planet we call home.

The New World represents a new way of thinking,

As opposed to the New World Order,

Which is rooted in outdated beliefs

That serve as a facade created by detached politicians,

Manipulative individuals, and greedy entrepreneurs

Who lament the little space left in their pockets

To stow away more corporations.

The world is weary of the old order,

Which changes names to favor a select few.

Let's forget history for a moment and focus on the present,

On the notions of imposed order.

Imagine a place where goodness prevails—

An Island of Hope in the desert of despair,

Where all hands and minds unite with shared goals.

BRIGHT MOMENTS

BRIGHT MOMENTS

There can be no forced inspiration,
But there can be mergers with the world,

There can be a flow of feelings,
Yet it can be overwhelming,

Flying outside to unite,
Flying inside to find

The melody of the moment,
When the yellow corona appears on the horizon

And another one across the mountain,
When the world turns mellow,

Hospitable and generous,
And you fly into the heart of the mountain

To find the egg of an unborn bird,
To break free and soar like a newborn eagle.

THIS IS SO SIMPLE

I sense the light within and around me.
The Sun is close and keen.

The world glows and I glow,
The world is expanding.

And I grow glowing,
Believing this is quite simple,

Not to think, but to glisten
Not to understand, but to feel

The light inside and outside
And grow by shining.

UNENDING LIFE

People often contemplate life after life.

Perhaps they believe there was no life before life,

Or perhaps they don't care about life before life.

Yet, if there were life before life,

There must be life beyond life.

If we existed before our birth,

We will be here even after we die.

But if there was no individuality before,

Why would it exist afterward?

It appears that this is not a matter of life

Or death, but a problem of ego

That does not accept the disappearance

Of individuality within the sea

Of an unending life for all.

AN OLD WOMAN

She relished fresh figs in the summer,

Gazing at their green skin,

Gently opening them

To savor the pink interior

Before consuming them.

During winter,

She savored dried figs and smoked fish,

Savoring them slowly

As if she learned it

From a Buddhist monk

On small joys.

Observing these rituals was enjoyable.

Not exactly eating

As for taking the necessary time.

POETRY AND LIFE

"Why poetry?" you ask.
Because of life, I respond.

Why love? Why hate? Why destruction?
Everything has a reason behind it.

The question of why always remains,
But there is a life that craves to be lived.

The answer to life is to live it,
And life itself does not require an answer.

TOO MUCH THINKING

His problem was that he was a deep thinker.

Excessive thinking can lead to paralysis.

While it inspires imagination,

Sometimes wild imagination

Loses touch with reality, creating projections

Of unimaginable and impossible desires.

This can feed the ego, causing it to grow too quickly,

Moving far ahead of its own steps

And straying from the path toward what is real.

It can often feel like arriving either too soon or too late.

Yet another question arises: do we truly know or understand

What is real or unreal, and what is too soon or too late?

NOES

When people want to be polite, they say, yes.
It is easy to reach an agreement while having fun.
And the same person who often says yes,
Often responds negatively when doing business.
Wit does not lead to approval.

WHO KILLED BEAUTY

You killed it!

How can I be sure?
I assisted you.
But now I feel ashamed,
Prepared for prosecution,
Ready to endure all consequences.
I want beauty back,
And you are cowards
For not admitting the crime.

HELL FROM THE HEART

Dark thoughts, dark images,
I cast spells on you.

I prefer to live with cheap sunsets
Rather than the rich descriptions of Hell!

Go away, dark thoughts,
Dark images, dark words,

Smuggled into the world
By the messengers of despair.

Go away, Hell!
I cast a spell on all of you.

If you return,
I will not rely solely on spells.

TOP OF THE MOUNTAIN IN THE MIDDLE OF THE STREET

THE
Summit
Seemed distant,
Yet it felt close and ordinary.
We loved visiting the mountains
But feared falling from the high cliffs.
These were not large mountains like Kilimanjaro,
But smaller ones filled with grass, spring flowers, and trees.
We attempted to ascend to the top and look down at the valley
And the city below, feeling as if we had reached the sky when we
stood
At the summit of the conquered Blue Mountain. However, we had
To make our way back down slowly and carefully to return
To the world in the valley and the bustling city,
More afraid of falling as we jumped down.
Some of us crawled to ensure a safe
Descent. We worried about those
Who seemed uncertain in their
MOVEMENT.

At one point, I fell from a small cliff and landed directly in the city street, surrounded by cars, hurried passengers, and pedestrians rushing as if they were trying to reach the top of the mountain I had just conquered. I fell back into the chaos of the busy world, feeling even more frightened after safely returning to the midst of it all.

CLEPSYDRA
I

what if a human civilization existed for about a million years,

or even one hundred million? What if there were only one

Homer every thousand years, one Dante in another

Thousand, and one Shakespeare in yet another?

That would amount to one thousand

Notable figures in a million years,

Or one hundred thousand

In one hundred million

Years. Who would

Be able to read

ALL

Of them

In a single lifetime,

Unless life were to be

Significantly extended in the future?

Perhaps there are civilizations like this

Scattered throughout the Universe, where beings

Can access the memories of their entire species. If we are

Fortunate, ours might become one of them. In such a scenario,

exceptional individuals like Homer, Dante, and Shakespeare could

Become more common and, as a result, might not receive the same

level of recognition they do now.

II

Perhaps this civilization would discover a way to condense and

Express ten or even one hundred times more thought in ten

Or one hundred times fewer words than we do now.

Or perhaps we would all become similar in

Knowledge but differ in desires, allowing

Us to avoid boredom as time progresses.

When the moment comes to navigate

This brief passage

And transition

INTO

A new realm of thinking

And understanding regarding

The human condition in the entire

Universe, or just on one planet, there might

Be an opportunity to construct a new temple, a new

Library in the heart of the Galaxy, perhaps even within

A black hole. This library could house the knowledge of

Angels or higher beings, and we might even enter a larger

Universe where our own is merely a minor planet or atom.

FEELINGS AND THOUGHTS

BEAUTY

It is beautiful to talk about beautiful things,
And even more beautiful to silently gaze at them.

It is beautiful to express love,
And even more beautiful to feel it.

Beauty is a cheap word
But beauty remains priceless.

UNUSUAL LOVE

You accepted my dreams, but I'm unsure if you accepted my
    thoughts.
You accepted conversations, but I'm unsure if you accepted ideas.
You accepted the words, but I'm unsure you understood the
    meanings.

This came long after the first hello,
Long after the turbulence of rough rides,
Long after accommodations and adjustments.

I have learned to accept your unusual ways,
Your intriguing thoughts on life, dreams, and the interplay between
    them.
I learned to accept your typical ways of expressing unusual desires.

Desires soared like birds in the morning,
When we are woken by the chimes of dreams,
Hypnotized and prepared for another round of living.

We would stroll down the street of a foreign city, mesmerized
By its history, recognized in the streets and gardens,
Filled with exotic flowers and grass—you loved the grass.

You loved green and blue.

You loved leaping into the water from the cliffs.

I have always felt afraid when you did that.

You mentioned you would teach me everything.

I never really found out what it was, but I agreed to be your

    student,

To learn whatever it may be.

You loved my mind and my words.

Other than that, you thought I could be complicated.

I have always known that nothing is easy

And accepted the ways of life, your uniquely typical ways,

And I lived a life I never thought I would.

It felt like a typhoon sweeping through paradise.

I thought I knew you

Although I can hardly see if I even knew myself.

That's how life often works.

What about psychology?

There is no way to analyze how a brain machine works,

The function of billions of cells, transmitters, and neurons

Flying, fighting, and competing.

How do ideas become reality?
That was yet another tricky question.

I could not find out anything about anything,
Except that I was alive and felt alive, yet I also felt dead;
I watched the rain, the fog, the horses, the birds, the trees, and the
    blue.

I enjoyed watching the blue every day.
You loved the same, though perhaps for different reasons;
Perhaps we loved each other for different reasons as well.

Did we hate each other?
I'm not sure. There were a few times when I felt hate towards you.
Did you hate me? Perhaps you did at times.

And perhaps you still hate me,
When you think of that July when blue was everywhere,
With the white dot in the middle shining like it was the first time,

When everything was lush,
And you were glistening at the center of it all—the blue, the green,
    the summer,
But I was not there for either love or hate.

FEELINGS AND THOUGHTS

Love flows abundantly within me.

I feel as if I might explode.

Then, "love less or open the window,"

Said the whisper in my mind or in the air.

YOU WILL NEVER LEAVE

No, you shall not leave.
You will remain here to dream with me.

No, you will not be leaving.
You will remain here to build a new home,

And even if you must leave,
You will always return home.

THE END OF THE PARTY

When she entered the room, she sensed trouble,

Although everything appeared to be in order.

The music played while people talked.

It was an ordinary party.

She stayed in the corner for a while, watching silently,

Pondering that strange feeling.

A man entered the room, walking past her,

Moving to the center of the room

Where there was a beautiful face with long blond hair

Shining above all the rest, giggling and

Talking. Bang, bang (she heard in the air).

That marked the end of the party.

WE WILL UNDERSTAND ONE ANOTHER

When those who traveled far return
And those who have never left begin to leave,
When memories are shared and understood,
We will understand each other.

When people with big ideas move to the corner,
And those in the corner move closer to the center.
When ideas are shared and comprehended,
Perhaps we will understand one another.

GOD AND LOVE

There are many unwritten histories and numerous religions,

But people usually adhere to just one.

According to monotheistic beliefs, there is only one God,

Yet numerous different texts exist about that same God.

We often prioritize the scriptures of our heritage

Over the universal God who serves all,

Regardless of our backgrounds and the poor choices

Made by fickle human beings.

There are different types of love,

And who can truly explain the major differences between them?

Countless lives have been lost

Over ideas about love and relationships,

But we often forget that the most important thing

Is to live and love.

Without living, life is worthless,

And love without living is lifeless.

There is life and there is existence.

The availability of love seems to be diminishing,

Regardless of the love offered from all directions.

Too many words attempt to replace the strong feelings

That were once felt most intensely in silence.

You once found happiness in that silence,

Even without fully understanding

Your emotions; it simply felt good.

There is everything and there is nothing.

When you love, everything exists,

And everything feels present.

In the absence of love,

There is a profound emptiness that fills your heart.

If you hate, everything feels dead,

And the entire world transforms

Into one immense void.

There are many religions,

But for the majority of believers, God is one.

There are many loves and many love stories,

But love is love, regardless of different experiences.

The only God worth believing in is the God of Love.

If there is a God, it must be Love.

The God of Love is Love itself.

If it is not Love God is not God.

Love is God and God is Love.

INSIDE AND OUTSIDE

It's difficult to be simple
When everything around is grand.
It's difficult to understand
When everything appears to be a mystery,
To love from a great distance,
To see inside while staying outside,
To pop a balloon, if that is all there is,
To discover a vast blue sky within,
To fly as far as your wings allow,
And dream that everything is much simpler
Than it appears from the outside.

UNPRETENTIOUS DREAMS

How difficult is it to refrain

From saying too much?

How difficult is it to love more—

To express simple ideas,

To live like a river gently eroding the stone,

To observe the distant spot from the shore,

To imagine places basking in its light,

Observe not just colors, shapes, or the sea,

But the simple life glistening

And hovering like a bird,

Filled with unpretentious dreams,

Satisfied solely with the ability to fly.

DO NOT COMPETE WITH THE SUN

Prune, but do not over-prune.

Shine, but don't compete with the Sun.

Beauty is indifferent to our desires.

It is as precise as a mathematical formula.

Don't strive to be an artist,

Be someone who embodies experience and trust.

Your concerns are often unfounded.

They originate from your ego, not from reality.

ADVICE FROM AN OLD MAN

Try not to be overly clever, and everything could turn out well.

Everything can be put in words, but not truly expressed.

There is beauty in words, but even more in hidden ones.

Love, scream, cry, hate, but never overkill.

Don't tell me you love me, make me believe you.

Don't say too much, but don't say too little either.

Balance is dictated more by sincerity than by craftsmanship.

I don't believe in prominent names; I only believe in facts.

When you find yourself, knock on my door.

If you wander too often, try to stay still for a moment.

Don't consider yourself too important, because you are not.

Don't fight for a place in history; fight for your place in life.

Don't tell me stories; pull me into the story and be a good host.

Don't try to seduce me with words; seduce me with their interplays
and happenings.

SILENT EQUALITY

BEST INTENTIONS

She bid a quick goodbye.
He stood there, speechless,
Frozen for a moment and taken aback,
Even though he had the best intentions
And hadn't done anything wrong.

AN IDEA

I cannot find the drawer
Where an old idea is preserved
In the universe of my mind.
Perhaps I never had an idea at all,
But only the concept of a concept—
A spark that suddenly ignited,
Or a memory of something
That never existed.

LATE WISDOM

I need to change my life,
But first, I must change myself,
And for that, it is too late.

FLYING AND MEDITATION

Meditation is beneficial occasionally,
But flying every day is even better.

MOUNTAINS AND SEAS

Mountains and seas
You exist within me

When I climb
To the top

Of the mind
Or dive deep

To the bottom
Of the heart

THE RETURN

I visited many exotic places,

Some very far away,

But I always returned to myself.

WONDER

Every day,

I wander and wonder

How peculiar

Everything around me seems.

It's strange to think

That I exist among it all,

Observing, inhaling its scent,

Hearing, touching,

Tasting, and feeling it

Every day.

STUPIDITY

When I want to remind myself of foolishness,
Especially my own, I switch on the TV.

BABY SQUIRREL

It walked in front of me on the sidewalk,
Barely the size of a mouse.
What are you doing here, poor little squirrel?
I watched it, fearing for its safety.

How did you get lost among people?
Far from the safety of your grassy home?
What was your mother doing?
Will anyone ever hold her accountable for neglecting you?

The squirrel shifted to the left,
Toward the entrance of a building, but the door was closed.
Then, it did what I feared—
It shifted to the right and found itself on the street.

As it reached the midpoint of the road,
Cars zoomed past. It attempted to turn back,
But I heard and saw nothing
Except for an SUV speeding by and other vehicles.

I believed it had a chance to return,
But time passed, and I could no longer see the little squirrel.

I returned to the street but found only

A tiny red mark on the pavement.

SILENT EQUALITY

It is impossible to say more than what is possible.

Unjustified ambition kills value and eats its own life,

Destroys another person's desire to soar,

Cuts their wings, and sucks in the air.

Get out, but avoid causing unnecessary accidents.

Nearly all of us believe we are clever,

And we all believe we are important,

But there is only so much space, only so much time,

Only so much desire, only as many words,

As few pages as possible, as little ink as necessary,

To accept all of us at light speed,

Hurrying into the Promised Land

Of oblivion, waiting for us sooner or later.

There is no reason for such a feverish rush,

For we shall arrive at the same place.

Justice will be served at the right time.

There will be neither better nor worse,

No distinctions between big and small,

No rewards, no punishment,

No guilt, no judgment, no hierarchies,

Only a silent equality.

SECRET OF LIFE

Perhaps the secret of life

Lies in not being too easy or too good,

To achieve the purpose effortlessly.

The purpose is always fleeting.

It is always the goal, almost equally distant

From when we started toward it.

Yet, there is always an invisible progression,

Slow and challenging to recognize;

It remains steady if we do not give in to weakness.

There is no perfect balance,

And within this imbalance lies the equilibrium

Of our efforts and achievements toward that purpose.

We call this pursuit the meaning of life.

While it can be challenging,

It may seem easier for those unwilling to fight for anything.

Success requires a willingness to pay the price.

BIG DREAMS

A MAN AND THE SEA: HOMAGE TO HEMINGWAY

It murmurs tirelessly, a forgotten song,

Telling the same story in the same way.

It listens to itself, indifferent to you,

Yet it charms and envelops you

With its music coming from afar.

It lulls you to sleep and then wakes you

With the same song, never tired

Of repeating its melody.

You go to the sea

To listen every morning,

Standing alone on the shore,

Inhaling the fresh scent

Of the ever-young and inviting world,

Happy to see you and greet you every time.

TEACHERS

We often disdain clichés,

Yet we pay a heavy price for them.

On television, in the streets,

In the Senate and classrooms,

Even in poetry,

Every word seems to be a cliché.

Neologisms aren't celebrated

Unless we view slang

As a new form of language.

Perhaps uniqueness

Resides in new combinations

Or in ordinary speech,

Transformed by extraordinary training

From a workshop

Led by an everyday enthusiast

Who, we must concede,

Has a profound love

For something that generates income,

Which supports a livelihood,

Even at the expense of what it is meant to teach.

LAZARONE

A wanderer through the streets, aimless and free,
No destination torments his soul.
Sometimes, while sitting on the curb, he becomes lost in thought.
At other times, he stands, watching the chaotic world.

A few coins fall softly from time to time.
There is no understanding between him and those around him.
To them, he's a disgrace, a shadow on their path,
While he sees them as lost souls chasing echoes.

In his reality, there is no journey from A to B,
Yet theirs is confined, wrapped tightly in routine.
He lacks freedom too, but wonders—can they not see?
Their chains are invisible, yet ever so present.

They call him a beggar; he views them with jest—
Professionals, each one, selling pieces of their lives.
To him, their labor is merely well-disguised stress,
While he embraces the art of simply being alive.

They think him a fool, a mere drifter in the dark,
But he carries a philosopher's heart within.

He knows that Diogenes would face similar scorn
If he wandered today beneath the same Sun's spin.

In cities like Rome or bustling New York,
They would cast their eyes down, seeing only the rags,
Missing the wisdom cloaked in simplicity,
Blind to the thoughts that dance beneath the labels.

So he carries on, a silent observer,
Finding beauty in moments most would dismiss.
In a world that rushes, he savors the still,
A question mark longing for answers in bliss.

EGOCENTRIC

How beautiful I am.

How grand my ideas are!

What I have accomplished and what I will achieve—

And what else could I do, if only they knew.

But he never understood who he referred to as "they."

He never realized that others could see

If there is beauty anywhere else—

If only he were aware.

BEAUTIFUL WORDS AND VANITY

I enjoy using beautiful words to express lovely thoughts,
Yet true beauty doesn't rely solely on elegant language,
Nor can it be conveyed entirely by it.
Often, it cries out for recognition in the somber corners of our
    minds.

Complicated words and complex ideas—
Illusions that spring from selfish dreams—
Eager to be acknowledged and celebrated,
Welcomed as profound insights rather than mere daydreams.

What sustains these illusions is nothing more than vanity.

PLACE OF BIRTH

Some believe they emerge from specific soil,
Others find their roots
Wrapped in the arms of a nation,
While some are encircled by kin or community.
Yet, some drift, untethered,
Without land, without lineage,
And without a name to call their own.

Every place can feel like a cage,
Every boundary is a chain—
Limiting the desire to stretch and soar.
But when you find your home
In every corner of the earth,
And every horizon feels familiar,
You come to realize:

There is no single territory,
No solitary tribe or nation
That can define your essence.
Instead, the world unfolds
As your cradle, your birthplace,
Where every heart beats
In rhythm with the universe.

In that vast embrace, you discover—

The whole world is your singular place of birth.

PERFECT BOREDOM

When there is noise and a crowd, trouble follows.

When everything is silent and perfect, it feels complete,

Yet there is nothing to fill the air but boredom.

BIG DREAMS

Much has already been said about many topics,

Yet our desire to express ourselves continues to grow.

What can we really say about this?

Speaking isn't always just about talking,

Growth isn't defined solely by progress,

And a strong desire alone isn't enough

To meet the expectations tied to unfulfilled dreams.

A PRAYER

Come to me, words,

Come to me, thoughts,

Come to me, songs,

I pray for your presence every day.

DEATH

Death is not death.

(At least not in a way people perceive it.)

If birth is a manifestation of life,

Then death is another manifestation.

Why concern ourselves with death?

Why pay more attention to death than to birth?

Just accept it without overthinking,

While living in the meantime.

Every thought about death

Takes away a moment of life.

LIFE IS POETRY

IMPERFECTION

Trying too hard to be too good,
Even when attempting to be bad,
It turns out too good for the bad,
And too bad for the good.

Perfection is often desired,
But it can feel sterile—
Final, with no mystery in it,
Like a product from an assembly line.

We wish for perfection,
Yet perfection is unachievable.
To attain perfect perfection,
A little touch of imperfection helps.

JUDGES AND ART

We don't have control over words;
This battle is already lost.
We can only use leftovers,
Assembling crumbs into music.
We think that clever arrangements
Are enough to create harmony.
We believe that a few lessons in prosody,
A decent knowledge of exotic words,
And some techniques for organizing everything
Are sufficient to make it seem
As if it comes from sincere inspiration and experience.
We assume this is enough to create real art,
Yet these artificial cacophonies,
Assembled as if they were symphonies,
Consist of words put together simply to be together—
Only because they sound good together
Or convey a certain idea about a supposed feeling.
Such works often attract the attention of judges,
Who serve as instant critics or measures
To assess the value of a product
Crafted to sound pleasant and convincing
Enough to be called art.
And for many, that is enough
To declare a historic victory.

ADVICES

Not seeking advice can lead to disaster.

Asking for advice might also turn out poorly.

Receiving unsolicited advice

Can be an even greater problem.

Finally, accepting and following advice

Without having requested it

Can be the worst disaster of all.

RECIPE FOR A DISASTER

When you try to be too clever,

Attempting to outsmart nature,

And challenging a God who remains indifferent,

You gain no value for yourself or the world.

Instead, by embracing who you are,

You at least have a chance, not to outsmart,

But to be on equal footing with yourself.

And that is worth striving for.

ETERNAL YOUTH IN MEMORY

When there is no loneliness,

Loneliness feels lonely,

Murmuring tirelessly the forgotten song.

Don't grow old, even as time passes,

Even when oblivion wraps you in its embrace.

Stay young, at least in your memories,

When every moment is squeezed into one.

As time flows, let the heart remember

The joy, the laughter, and the dreams,

For in these echoes lies eternal youth.

LIFE IS POETRY

Good poets are good copy editors.

AMATEURS

There is no better or worse;
It's all a matter of taste.

BANANAS

Brother liked bananas.

If there were fifteen bananas,

And he was alone,

He would still leave two for us.

DOGS AND MEN

When a dog makes a friend,

It's a certainty.

When a man makes a friend,

It's unpredictable.

SAYING GOODBYE

To say or not to say more,

That is the question.

As I reflect now,

I've shared all I needed to express,

And have nothing more to add,

Except to say goodbye.

ABOUT THE AUTHOR

Dejan Stojanović (1959) was born in Peć, Kosovo (formerly part of Serbia, Yugoslavia). Although he received a legal education, he has never practiced law. Instead, he became a journalist and foreign correspondent in the early 1990s; however, he is primarily a poet, essayist, philosopher, and businessman.

He has published the following poetry collections:

Circling (Krugovanje), Narodna knjiga—Alfa, Belgrade, published in three editions: 1993, 1998, and 2000.
The Sun Watches Itself (Sunce sebe gleda), NIP Književna reč, Belgrade, 1999.
The Sign and Its Children (Znak i njegova deca), Prosveta, Belgrade, 2000.
The Creator (Tvoritelj), Narodna knjiga, Belgrade, 2000.
The Shape (Oblik), Gramatik, Podgorica, 2000.
The Dance of Time (Ples vremena), Konras, Belgrade, 2007.

Pentalogy: *The World in Nowherness (Svet u nigdini)*, Udruženje književnika Srbije, Belgrade, 2017:
(1) *Ozar (Ozar)*,
(2) *The World and God (Svet i Bog)*,
(3) *The World in Nowhereness (Svet u nigdini)*,
(4) *The World and Humans (Svet i ljudi)*,
(5) *The Home of Light (Dom svetlosti)*.

The Hidden Light (Skrivena svetlost), Čigoja, Belgrade, 2018.
Primordial Spark (Iskra iskona), Albatros plus, Belgrade, 2021.
Centuries and Steps (Vekovi i koraci), Albatros plus, Belgrade, 2023.

Essays:

Creator and Creating (Stvaralac i stvaranje), Albatros plus, Belgrade, 2021.

The New Man and the New World (Novočovek i novosvet), Rad, Belgrade, 2022.

Anthology: *Selected Serbian Plays* (*Izabrane srpske drame*), USA, 2016.

A book of his selected interviews, *Conversations* (*Razgovori*), was published in 1999 by NIP Književna reč in Belgrade. The Serbian Heritage Foundation and the Association of Writers of Serbia for Intellectual Engagement awarded the book the Rastko Petrović Prize.

Collected Poems: 1978-2000 (Pentalogy 1), New Avenue Books, 2025 (Translation from Serbian).

Books written in English:

Philosophy: *Absolute,* New Avenue Books, USA, 2024.

Poetry Series: *The Embrace of Light and Darkness* (Pentalogy 3):
- *Dance of Sounds*, New Avenue Books, 2025
- *The Matter of Matter*, New Avenue Books, 2025
- *The Home of the World*, New Avenue Books, 2025
- *All Women in One*, New Avenue Books, 2025
- *The Light of the Mind*, New Avenue Books, 2025

He lived in Chicago, USA, from 1990 to 2014, and holds citizenship in both Serbia and the United States.

www.ingramcontent.com/pod-product-compliance
Lightning Source LLC
Chambersburg PA
CBHW052013240626
47153CB00008B/2855